Wizard Gold

First published in 2008
by Wayland

This paperback edition published in 2009

Text copyright © Anne Cassidy 2008
Illustration copyright © Martin Remphry 2008

Wayland
338 Euston Road
London NW1 3BH

Wayland Australia
Hachette Children's Books
Level 17/207 Kent Street
Sydney, NSW 2000

Series Editor: Louise John
Cover design: Paul Cherrill
Design: D.R.ink
Consultant: Shirley Bickler

A CIP catalogue record for this book is available from the British Library.

ISBN 9780750251839 (hbk)
ISBN 9780750251846 (pbk)

Printed in China

Wayland is a division of Hachette Children's Books,
an Hachette Livre UK Company

www.hachettelivre.co.uk

Wizard Gold

Written by Anne Cassidy
Illustrated by Martin Remphry

WAYLAND

Wizard Wizzle was casting a spell.

He was trying to turn a frog into a prince!

"Oh no!" said his sister, Wanda,
"There are frogs everywhere!"

The king came into the magic
chamber. He stamped his feet and
shook his fists.

"Where is my wizard?"
he shouted.

"Your majesty, what's wrong?"
asked Wanda.

The king took Wizzle and Wanda to his treasure chest.

"Look!" he cried. "All my gold has disappeared."

"I will help," said Wizzle, "I will use my magic to find the gold."

13

Wizzle cast a spell. Wanda gave him a dog's hair, some parrot feathers and an elephant's tooth.

He put them into a huge glass bowl
and waved his magic wand.

"Izzle, Wizzle, Woo! Show me
where the king's gold has gone!"
he commanded.

The glass bowl began to sparkle and fizz. Then a funny creature appeared.

It had a wagging tail, red wings
and an elephant's trunk!

Oh dear! Another spell had
gone wrong.

The king was very angry. He stamped his feet and pulled his hair.

"You're a hopeless wizard!" he
shouted. "Put him in the dungeon!"

The king's soldiers took Wizzle to
the dungeon and bolted the door.

In the dungeon, Wizzle got to work making new spells. He had to find out where the gold was.

Wanda watched him and sighed. She knew it was up to her now.

The next day, Wanda was watching the king's jester doing tricks.

Suddenly, Wanda saw something fall from his pocket.

It was a gold coin. Had the jester stolen the king's gold?

Wanda tiptoed after the jester.

He went down the stairs into
a secret room in the darkest part
of the castle.

Wanda peeped around the door.
There was the king's gold!

Wanda ran to find the king. "Wizard Wizzle knows where your gold is!" she shouted.

The king unlocked the door of the
dungeon and let Wizzle out.

He followed Wizzle and Wanda
down the stairs and opened the door
of the secret room. Inside was
all the king's gold...

...and the jester!

"Take that jester to the dungeon!"
shouted the king.

"Maybe you're not such a bad wizard after all," he said, smiling at Wizzle.

START READING is a series of highly enjoyable books for beginner readers. They have been carefully graded to match the Book Bands widely used in schools. This enables readers to be sure they choose books that match their own reading ability.

The Bands are:

| Pink / Band 1 |
| Red / Band 2 |
| Yellow / Band 3 |
| Blue / Band 4 |
| Green / Band 5 |
| Orange / Band 6 |
| Turquoise / Band 7 |
| |
| Gold / Band 9 |

START READING books can be read independently or shared with an adult. They promote the enjoyment of reading through satisfying stories supported by fun illustrations.

Anne Cassidy has written lots of books for children. Many of them are about talking animals who get into trouble. She has two dogs, Charlie and Dave, but, sadly, neither of them talk to her! This time she wanted to write about a funny wizard who gets his spells mixed up.

Martin Remphry grew up on the tiny Channel Island of Sark. He has always loved drawing, especially spooky things such as witches and wizards, so it was a dream come true for him to illustrate Wizzle. He loves the funny ingredients Wizzle uses for his spells, even if they don't always work as he hopes!